To Miia,
Happy Reading!
Kathy Nunn
Vasconcellos

Carmen
and His
Animal Friends

Kathy Nunn Vasconcellos
Author and Illustrator

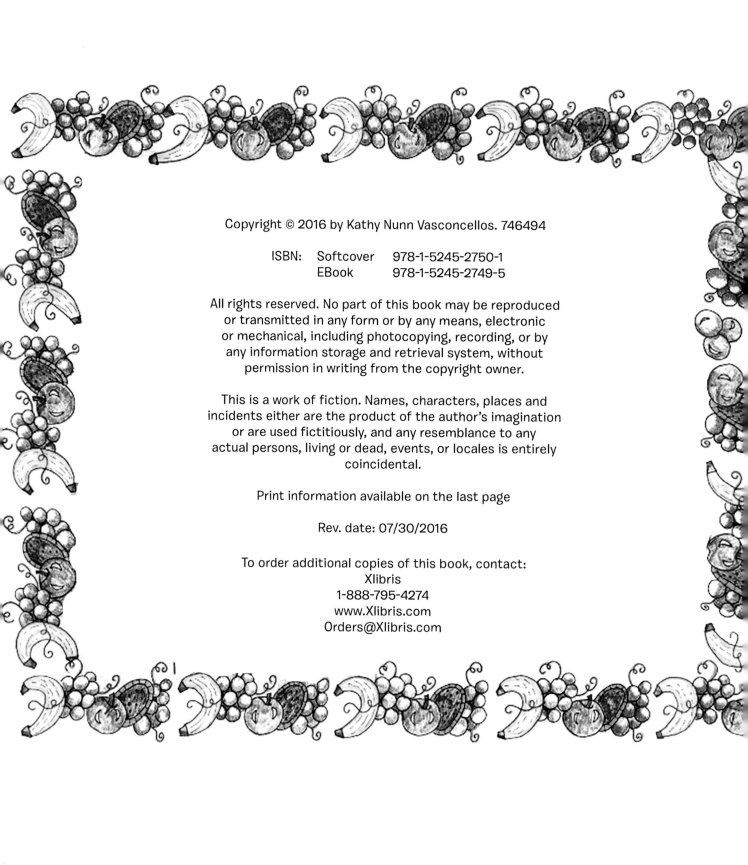

Print information available on the last page

Rev. date: 07/30/2016

To order additional copies of this book, contact:
Xlibris
1-888-795-4274
www.Xlibris.com
Orders@Xlibris.com

DEDICATION

I would like to dedicate this
book to my loving family.

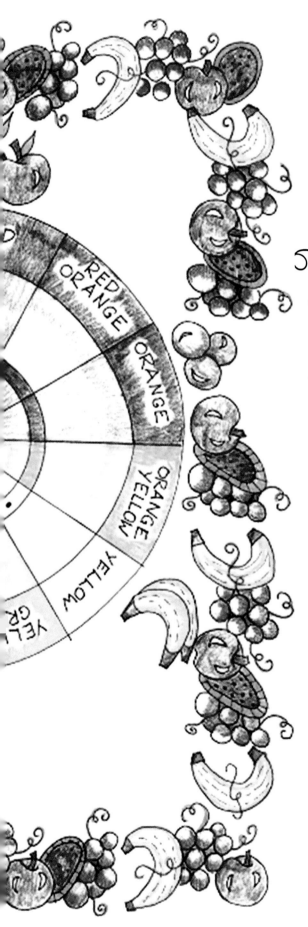

This is a story about Carmen the Chameleon. He has many animal friends. Some walk, some fly, some slither and some even climb trees! Throughout Carmen's travels he makes even more animal friends. Their coats, skin and feathers are made up of beautiful colors.

What colors do you know?

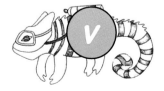

The first animals that Carmen visits are in a jungle. He can see a brown monkey and a green frog, a toucan with a big orange beak and even a yellow cheetah taking a peek!

What other objects can you find in the picture?

All of a sudden the room becomes loud! Beautiful birds and ducks are squawking to each other quite proud! Some quack and some cackle, oh what a scene! Some of their feathers are red, orange and green!

What is your favorite kind of bird? Do you know what your state bird is? What colors are their feathers?

All at once it's quiet again. Carmen wants to take a nap with his furry friend. She is lying on a shelf in the library. Her colors are browns and tan, her coat is warm and fuzzy. Carmen lays down quietly so as not to disturb her sleep. Once he closes his eyes he starts dreaming of sheep!

What is it like when you go to a library? What kind of books do you like to read?

Next Carmen comes face to face with a beautiful purple and green peacock in the Zoo. The peacock stares at Carmen with angry eyes. Maybe Carmen should wear a disguise! Carmen's colors change to magenta and purple too. He walks carefully through the cages and sees many animals, both old and new.

Have you ever seen a peacock? What colors were the feathers?

The leaves are falling down on the farm. The scarecrow keeps them all safe and sound. Carmen walks among cows, rabbits, dogs and a donkey. The farm animals have fun roaming around. There's even a duck and a big blue and yellow truck. The cow lays in the pasture, her spots are black. She knows every animal both forward and back.

Have you ever been to a farm? What was it like? Did you see a truck or a tractor? Have you ever milked a cow?

In the forest there is lots of noise. There's a deer, a squirrel, a groundhog and Tom Turkey. The birds in the air are keeping it perky! A cabin in back of the forest is somewhere to go. But we don't want Mr. Skunk to steal the show!

Have you seen a log cabin or been in one? Was it warm or cold? What colors did you see?

Next Carmen puts on his gear and jumps into the ocean! His stripes turn into orange and blue. He swims among turtles, fish, frogs and lobster, all in a beautiful color and hue. There's even a grand sand castle where fish swim in and out. He's having lots of fun there isn't a doubt!

Do you have a fish aquarium at home that looks like this? Are there plants and rocks at the bottom?

Carmen takes a dive from the highest branch to the hive. He comes across beautiful winged butterflies and enormous bees! They are making lots of honey close to the trees. He hopes that they will share their sweet nectar with him. He takes a big swallow and jumps out on a limb!

Have you ever seen a beehive? Was it scary? Have you tasted honey?

Once again Carmen returns to the jungle where it's hot and funky. He encounters a large elephant, some giraffes and a monkey. There are also beautiful green leaves and pink flowers. Carmen could sit and watch them for hours.

What do you think it would be like to live in a jungle? What other things do you see in this picture?

A hop, skip and jump and Carmen's in the desert. He sees a ram, some boars, jackrabbits and the iguana. The cactus are the best, though, bright green with yellow flowers. He also sees some jackrabbits with legs full of power!

What do you think it would be like to live in the desert? Do you think the temperature is hot? What about the prickly cactus?

BRRRR! It sure is cold up here in the arctic! Carmen gets to know polar bears and penguins. They love the cold air and snow. He even sees a gray whale tail coming up through the ice! The baby penguins catch him some fish. Don't you know that fish are his favorite dish?

Do you like cold weather and snow? What about snow days?

"Home is where the heart is," as they say. The end of Carmen's travels is coming up fast. He has enjoyed making lots of new animal friends, such a blast!

Finally, Carmen meets his new best friend, Carmella. He is so happy and grateful and one lucky fella!

Hope you have enjoyed his colorful adventures!

Edwards Brothers Malloy
Thorofare, NJ USA
August 10, 2016